SONIC™
THE HEDGEHOG

SONIC AND THE TALES OF TERROR

PENGUIN YOUNG READERS LICENSES
An Imprint of Penguin Random House LLC

Cover illustration by Ian McGinty

ISBN 9781524787318
10 9 8 7 6 5 4 3 2 1

SONIC™
THE HEDGEHOG

SONIC AND THE TALES OF TERROR

by Kiel Phegley
illustrated by Patrick Spaziante

Penguin Young Readers Licenses
An Imprint of Penguin Random House

NIGHT OF THE UNLIVING

The heroes stood frozen in the eerie
green light of the machine.
The saucer-like monster
hovered in the glade. But
aside from the strange
lights that pulsated
from its dome head,
the thing had simply
hummed a low
sound since appearing
mysteriously outside the city.

"Maybe it just wants to make friends," said Big the Cat. The gentle giant reached out a hand toward the saucer's body.

"Be careful," said Tails, hovering over the scene on the twin helicopter blades that gave him his name. "You don't know what—"

ZAAAANG!

It was too late. The moment Big touched the machine, an awful grinding noise emanated from within. The massive metal monster spun around and bore itself into the ground.

"Submit or be destroyed!" cried a hollow, angry voice from within.

"Well, I think that settles that!" Amy ran up from the edge of the glade and called to her team. "Big! Cream! Let's give it a little flower power!" Without a word, Big opened up his large bamboo umbrella and twirled it over his head. Amy and Cream the Rabbit jumped on top, holding each other's hands and whipping up a furious spinning speed.

"One, two, three . . . GO!" Amy called and then let go of Cream to shoot herself at the machine with full force. Her hammer swung around in midair for a mighty blow, and then . . . *Clang!* Amy bounced straight off the whirling body of the saucer! She hit the dirt and rolled to safety, but the machine continued its awful dig, sinking its body firmly into the earth.

"Submit! Submit! Submit!" it called out in a droning tone that set the heroes' hairs on end.

"It looks like the top may be vulnerable!" yelled Tails over the noise. "Try to crush its dome!"

SWOOOSH!

In a split second, a blue blaze flew over their heads, nearly blowing the heroes down with its force. The spinning ball of fury shot toward the machine's dome like a bullet and struck it hard and true. The dome crumpled as the blue blur came into focus as Sonic the Hedgehog.

"Were you waiting long? Just kidding. I know you weren't," he said with a smirk, and crouched to balance.

Underneath him the half-sunken saucer shivered and steamed. "Submit! Submit! Submmmmmm . . . ," it wheezed before finally splitting wide open. With a wet, sickening sound, the metal body of the monster burst, shooting a torrent of sticky green slime all over Amy's team.

"Whoa!" said Tails as he zipped high in the air to miss the green goo.

"Gross!" called Amy. "I feel like I got sneezed on by a giant."

"Oh, my poor Cheese!" said Cream, picking up

8

her floating sidekick pal from where he was knocked to the ground.

"Oh, I don't know," said Big, sitting calmly in the squishy green slime. "It actually feels kind of . . . nice."

"Hahahaha!" laughed Sonic. "Sorry to say, but that's what happens when you're not the fastest thing alive."

Without the robotic saucer body, all that was left of the machine was a tall metal spire. In its middle sat a large green meteor rock that continued to pulsate with strange light, even as it dripped the disgusting discharge.

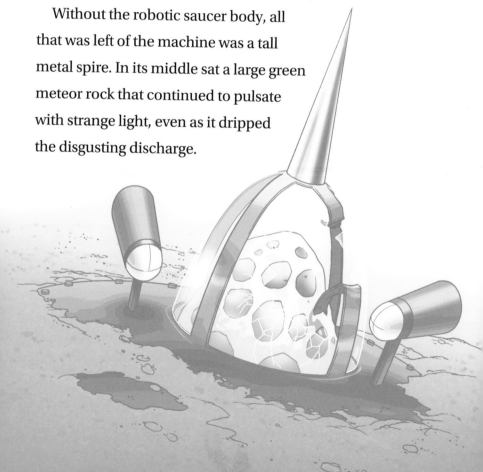

"We'll have to contact a medical team to decontaminate you," Tails said. "Standard procedure."

"Have fun waiting to get hosed off," said Sonic as he swung outside the slime radius with Tails' help. "I've got more action to find instead of getting stuck in place."

The next day, Sonic sped through town in search of some fun. Street after street, the scene was calm and quiet. No explosions or attacks or action of any kind. Except at . . . Cream and Cheese's house?

Out front, the kindly rabbit and her partner were making a racket of clangs from a mountain of sheet metal. Cream struck a large wrench against the warped pile again and again. Sparks flew each time she struck, some jumping into Cheese's eyes. But neither of them seemed to care.

"Uh, hey, Cream," Sonic said as he skidded into her driveway. "Working on an art project?"

"We are building the spear," said the rabbit without stopping.

"Right, the spear . . ." Sonic didn't know exactly what to

say. "And you think a wrench is going to shape that metal up the way you want?"

Cream stopped her motion mid-swing. She pulled the tool down slowly and stared at it for a long moment. The quiet made Sonic uncomfortable. "Perhaps you are right," she said at last.

The wrench dropped with a thud, and Cream reached up her hands to grab the metal firmly. With surprising strength and an agonizing squeaking sound, the rabbit folded two pieces of strong metal together as though they were paper. She started to mold and shape the pile like clay.

"Wow!" said Sonic. "Have you been working out?"

The little Chao creature that followed Cream everywhere floated up to Sonic's nose. "Chao."

Cream explained to Sonic that this meant they had been strengthened and wanted Sonic to join them.

"Um . . . I've got somewhere else to be," Sonic said and sped away before he got too close.

The strange encounter drove Sonic across the city to Amy's home. If anyone knew what was going on with those two, it would be their best friend. But when Sonic arrived,

Amy didn't charge out to greet him.

"Amy? Anyone home?" Sonic called into the curiously open door. When no one answered, he walked in—carefully, in case there was an ambush waiting. But what he found was almost too boring: Amy and a room of maps.

"This planet has so many people on it," she said without looking up. Amy leaned over a massive map of the planet. Pinned on every wall were charts of country borders and city streets. She was totally absorbed.

"Planning a trip?" Sonic asked and forced a flat chuckle.

"The trip is over," she said slowly. "All that's left now is to . . . ah, ah, AH-CHOO!" Amy sneezed, covering her mouth with her hand, but Sonic noticed that her hands were now covered in green slime!

"Gross!" said Sonic.

Amy just looked at him with an empty stare. She slowly reached out her slime-covered hands. "It's fine," she said. "Touch it and you'll see."

In a blur, Sonic was gone again, roaming the streets for answers to whatever had happened to his friends. No matter how fast he ran, no answers came. Then it hit him. The slime! The crash site must hold the answers to what was happening.

Within seconds, Sonic was back on the outskirts of town and rushing into the quiet glade. What met him there was another friend. Or was it?

Big sat still as a stone in the blackened pit that the saucer had dug. While his back was to Sonic, it was clear the large purple cat was staring up at the dented meteorite that still glowed an eerie shade of green.

"Hey, pal," Sonic called, trying to sound normal. "Fish ain't biting today?"

"Fish?" Big finally said. "No! We are busy!" He rose slowly like a sleeping giant and lurched around. His eyes had turned a bright green, and streams of green goo dripped down them into his whiskers.

"To understand us," said the cat slowly, "all you . . . have to do . . . is submit."

They couldn't be talked to. They couldn't be fought. And they most definitely couldn't be touched. Sonic sprinted in a

panic, thinking how he might save his pals . . .

"Tails!" Sonic burst into his friend's lab. "We need to do something! That space probe robot has infected Amy, Big, Cream, and Cheese with some kind of virus!"

"But that's not possible," said Tails. "The medical team

checked the entire site. There was no organic matter in that robot. Even that green slime was just some kind of insulation."

"I don't care what you call it. It did a number on our friends, and now they're acting like some kind of creepy crawlies," said Sonic. He paced the room. "What can we do?"

"Well, I am running some tests on this sliver of meteorite," Tails said as he pulled back a shelf to reveal a two-inch chip of the rock. Sonic stopped dead in his tracks when he saw the green glare of the fragment.

"Tails . . . you didn't touch it, did you?"

"Of course not!" said the fox. "There's still a chance a metal like this could be highly volatile, so I took every precaution extracting it from the crash."

"Well, we've got to figure out what it is and fast!" said Sonic. He looked out at the streets from the window. In the distance he thought he could see Cream, slowly trudging along with a massive metal spike slung over her shoulder.

"That's easier said than done," said Tails. "I'm good, but I'm no expert in cosmic metallurgy. I'm afraid we're just going to have to wait until I can run every test I know."

But in the street, people were starting to scream. Cream began using her flying ability with her ears to spread slime all over the town. People were getting infected by the green slime and slowly turning into a diseased mob, wandering around in slow motion as Tails and Sonic watched in horror.

"Tails," he said. "If there's one thing I'm bad at, it's waiting."

The evening became a nightmare in slow motion. Sonic left Tails locked up in the lab and hit the town at top speed, warning anyone and everyone to avoid the sick. But no matter how fast Sonic ran, he was always too late.

The people of the city were shambling through the streets. Their heads hung low, and their eyes glowed with sticky green slime. Yet despite their lethargic motions, everyone's strength seemed to have increased tenfold. They tore up street lamps and stop signs and mailboxes. Anything metal was ripped up, crunched together, and carried away by the groaning masses.

"Submit," they droned on as each new piece of steel was dragged away. *"Submiiiiiiiit."*

"They're building something," Sonic said as he zipped along the alleys of the city undetected.

Suddenly, a city bus landed in the street ahead of Sonic with an epic BOOM! He skidded hard to avoid hitting it. When Sonic looked up, he saw Big lumbering toward him.

"Why does it run from us?" Big said. "We will not hurt it."

Sonic spun to run the other way only to see Cream and Cheese approaching from across the street.

"Chao?" said Cheese in a hollow voice.

Sonic backed up against the wall of a building only to see Amy slinking along the curb toward him. Her face was an eerie green mask.

"Why can't it realize that it must submit," she said, raising a hand, "or be DESTROYED!"

Sonic sprinted through a small opening between two of them, and as he raced away he looked back at an army of droning people with glowing green eyes.

"They're right behind me, Tails!" said Sonic as he slid into the lab.

The fox pulled an emergency lever. The windows and doors of the lab were soon covered by metal doors four feet thick. "I built this in case Eggman ever attacked, but it should hold them back for now," he said.

"But what are we going to do about them? They're everywhere!"

Tails sat at his workshop bench and rubbed his eyes. "I have an idea," he said as a schematic of the saucer machine lit up on a screen behind him. "The green meteorite is more than a mere power source. It has a mind of its own."

Outside, the army of the infected had reached Tails' lab and began scratching at the metal walls. *Scritch, scritch, scriiiiiiiitch.*

"So it's some kind of alien invader?" asked Sonic as the sound grew louder.

"Not exactly. This thing isn't living or dead," Tails said in awe. "It's more like a computer than anything else. Sailing through space on a makeshift craft for thousands of years. It's like a spear thrown into the sky that never came down. A spear with a simple, primitive program driving it: to take over all it comes into contact with."

"So if it's not alive or dead, how do we stop it?" said Sonic as the *scritch, scritch* seemed to crawl up his spine.

"I built this amplifier," Tails said, holding up a large circuit board brimming with wires. "It's attuned to the meteorite's unique frequency. I've used it to 'speak' to the fragment."

"And?!?" Sonic clenched his teeth.

"It's amazing, really," said Tails as he stared at the green fragment, encased in a glass container. "Just imagine! Traveling in the cold of space for millennia. It's slower than us, but so much more patient. We can't even begin to understand what it can do, how it can communicate . . . through touch and transmission and even by sight. And once we amplify it fully, everyone will understand."

Scritch, scritch, scritch. Tails began rubbing his nails against the glass slowly.

"Buddy, what are you talking about?" Sonic said as he reeled back in horror.

Tails turned to his friend as two thin green tears ran down his face. "Don't fight us anymore, Sonic," he said. "We've waited this long. We will take you eventually. And it's so much nicer once you submit . . ."

With a slow squeeze, the fox shattered the glass container, grasped the meteorite fragment in his hand, and slammed down hard on the security switch. *Scritch. Scratch. SCROOOM!* In an agonizing instant, endless streams of green arms scratched their way into the raising doors and lunged at Sonic.

Sonic swooped through the lab and stole away Tails' amplifier device. Within seconds, he slipped through a rare unclogged window and sprinted for the hills.

"They need this thing to complete whatever they've got planned," said Sonic as he ran into the night. "But what can I do that doesn't just slow them down?"

Fortunately for Sonic, Tails had prepared a memo that he now noticed was attached to the amplifier, telling him exactly what he needed to do!

>>>>>>>>>

In the black of midnight, Amy, Tails, and the rest of the
infected wandered their way to the crash site and handed
their metal over to Big. Twice as strong as the others, he

24

molded their collection around the meteorite's spire to create one massive broadcast tower.

"We have found the path," Big said in a robotic tone.

"We will send the signal home and call the great meteor here," said Cream, staring up at the tower.

"And soon, this entire planet will submit to us," said Amy.

"Or be destroyed?" called Sonic. He stood on a branch high above the crowd with the amplifier in his hands, and they turned their heads slowly in unison to look at him.

"Do you understand us now?" called Tails. "That we can wait forever to win?"

"I've accepted the reality," said Sonic. "So, I figured I might as well speed things up."

He leaped from the tree, holding Tails' amplifier above his head, and landed in the green crowd. Their hands were all over him as they passed Sonic across the glade. Each new touch rubbed him in slime, and he soon started to hear a voice in his head.

"Submit," it whispered. "Join us and be strong in the cold stillness of time."

By the time Sonic had been passed to the

metal tower, his eyes were bleary with the green light. Its power coated his brain, overriding any impulse that was his own. It would be easy to give in, but his mind raced with a plan.

"This . . . ," Sonic said slowly, handing forward the device, "this will . . . spread our message . . . across the stars . . ."

Big the Cat lifted Sonic up, and the hedgehog pressed the amplifier onto the tower just above the glowing green meteorite. The crowd swayed in excitement. Sonic felt as if his brain was drowning. Did he really want to do this? Did he want to submit to the power of the unliving rock?

His hands attached the wires of Tails' creation to the tower slowly. His fingers ran over its dials, sticking on the buttons. Finally it was ready.

"I . . . I'm sorry," said Sonic as he flipped a switch on.

And then his vision erupted in fire.

The world came into focus as the light of day stung Sonic's eyes. He was in a hospital bed, surrounded by . . .

"Tails! Amy! Big!" Sonic cried as he kicked off the covers.

"It's okay, Sonic," said Amy. "We're cured!"

He relaxed and sunk into the bed. "So it worked?"

"I'm glad that you found my memo," said Tails. "Overloading the amplifier created a wicked feedback loop. The meteorite's power was never meant to pump out that much info that quickly."

"Gotta move fast," Sonic laughed to himself. "But was anyone hurt?"

"Just you, pal," said Tails. "When the machine overloaded, it sparked and caught fire in your hands. Luckily, the feedback was enough to burn the program out of everyone's system and melt down the tower."

Sonic looked down at his hands. They were fully wrapped in clean white gauze and throbbing in pain.

"Will I be okay?" he asked.

"You will make a full recovery," said Big. "All it will take is time and patience."

"Ugh!" said Sonic. "If there's one thing I'm bad at, it's waiting!"

SPOOK FOREST

The smoke of the campfire rose up into the branches of the forest like a ghostly apparition. Sonic the Hedgehog leaned into the popping of the burning logs, lifting his hands to make spidery shadows across his friends' faces.

"And the disembodied hand reached up," he said. "And pushed the camper off the cliff and into oblivion!"

"Ahhhh!" shouted the heroes around the fire before breaking into laughter. For two nights, Team Sonic had hosted their allies from the team called Chaotix to sleep out under the stars in the ancient forest. And what was a good campout without scary stories?

"That one was good, but I don't think anything can top Vector's story about the mummy DJ," said Charmy Bee as he buzzed around the fire.

"Naw, Espio's story about the invisible truck driver scared me silly," said Vector the Crocodile, his headphones for once turned off for some peace and quiet.

"Don't you mean," called a voice from the edge of the gathering, "Bubba the Unseen!" Espio the Chameleon

faded into sight just behind his croc pal with his fingers forming the hook hands of the spectral trucker.

"You guys are a bunch of dopes!" called Knuckles the Echidna from a stump away from the campfire. Though Sonic had invited his team along to help build friendships between the two groups of heroes, the prickly Knuckles spent most of the weekend with his arms crossed.

"Come on, Knuck," Sonic called as he plucked a hot dog off a stick. "Get into the spirit of a spooky evening."

Knuckles stomped across to the others with a cross look. "There ain't no such thing as spooks or ghouls or ghosts. We've got enough problems in this world fighting off Eggman's robots, alien invaders, and creatures from beyond the universe. There's no reason to drum up kids' tales about graveyard spirits on top of all that."

"Now, Knuckles," said Tails. "Some say that ghost stories represent a battle within ourselves that we haven't won yet. You could learn something from them."

"That's bunk!" said Knuckles and crossed his arms again.

"You know what I think?" said Sonic with a mischievous grin. "I think Knuckles has got an old-school case of the willies! He's afraid of the things that go 'Boo!' in the night."

"Yeah!" laughed Vector. "Fearless leader maybe ain't so fearless after all, haw-haw!"

With that, Knuckles' eyes went wide with fury. "Afraid?!? I'm the bravest, toughest thing any of you chumps has ever seen. And I'll prove it!" He stormed off into the darkness.

Sonic's face dropped as his friend walked away. "Aw, come on, Knuckles!" he called. "I didn't mean anything by it!" But the echidna was already far off in the distance.

"Don't worry, Sonic," said Espio. "That loner just needs to blow off some steam. Anyway, what could hurt him out here?"

In the blackness of the forest, Knuckles let out his anger on the silent trees.

"Afraid! What a bunch of baloney!" he said and swiped his fist against the trunk of an old oak tree. A chunk of wood and bark went flying as his punch left a jagged scar. "Look at that. There's nothing I can't fight my way out of."

Then, in the silence of the forest, Knuckles heard a sharp crack, followed by a thundering thump.

"What the—?" He spun around, but saw nothing.

Again, a painful cracking sound echoed across the night, followed by an earth-shaking crash.

"Who goes there?!" he cried out. "Show yourself, you cowards!"

Just then, a sound like breaking bones assaulted Knuckles' ears, and he turned, realizing that it was the shattering of a tree's roots that caused it. Before he could think, the mighty trunk before him shivered and sunk into the ground with a violent boom. The forest floor shook, and Knuckles was knocked to the ground.

"How in the world did that happen?" he said, jumping to his feet. As he looked closer, he heard a deep grinding noise, and a long, red metal tail slithered out of sight. "It's Dr. Eggman! He's built some kind of new machine, and it's digging its way toward Sonic, Tails, and the Chaotix!"

Knuckles raced on his feet in the direction of the robo-digger. Out ahead of him, every few minutes another tree would shiver, crack, and get swallowed whole into the earth. As he ran through the path of destruction, Knuckles realized he'd been turned around during the chase. "Isn't it just like the gang to go and get lost when I'm trying to help them!" he said.

Then, in the distance, a massive tree rose up into Knuckles' vision. It reached so high into the sky that it felt like the branches might grab onto the moon and not let go. Its trunk was as thick as a building, with bumps and grooves all along it that looked almost like sad, agonized faces. At its base, the tree's roots bubbled up above the dirt and made a tangled web of trip wires for fifty yards all around.

As he approached it, Knuckles felt this was less a tree and more some kind of massive living monster.

Behind him, he heard another crack and rumble.

"You're not getting this tree, Eggman," said Knuckles. "Not today."

The echidna sprinted away from the tree and directly toward danger. Nearly two hundred yards out, he felt the vibrations of the metal monster approaching. He jumped high in the air and punched down into the ground with epic force, sending shock waves through the dirt. A moment later, Knuckles could hear the whirring gears of the machine in the distance. It was retreating.

"I've kept it at bay for now," he said. "But if I don't . . ."

Before he could finish the thought, the ground beneath him began to rumble. Knuckles' feet sank into the dirt as the forest floor began to swirl around him like a whirlpool. And then it opened up and swallowed him whole, pulling him deep, deep down into the ground, like a hand from beyond the grave.

Back at the campsite, the fire had burned down low into a pile of glowing embers. Sonic and Tails sat up in their sleeping bags, talking.

"Do you think Knuckles is all right?" Sonic said.

"You know he's always been a lone wolf . . . or, you know, a lone echidna," said Tails. "I'm sure he'll show up when he's ready."

"I know, I know." Sonic sighed. "I just felt bad. This was supposed to be fun. I didn't bring us here to fight."

"He'll get over it, Sonic." The fox yawned. "It's not like

Knuckles hasn't been known to sling a few cheap shots in his day. Just enjoy the peace and quiet."

Just then, the forest all around them began to ring with a horrible cracking sound. Ancient wood turned to splinters to the left, to the right . . . everywhere! And the ground began to shake and tilt on the edges of the clearing.

"Wha. . . what the heck is happening?" cried Charmy as he flew down from the tree he'd been snoozing in.

"We're being attacked!" said Espio.

"*Zzzzzzzz* . . . ," snored Vector, on the ground with his noise-canceling headphones pumping jams in his ears.

"Get him up!" said Sonic. "Everyone form a circle!"

The combined teams soon stood shoulder-to-shoulder around the rock-protected fire pit. Suddenly, the trees on the edges of the clearing were sucked into the ground. The heroes' heads snapped all around, but they still couldn't see who was behind it all.

"Is it a g-g-g-ghost?!?" asked Charmy.

"I'm betting it's more like a ghoul . . . named Eggman!" said Sonic.

At that very moment, a metal dome burst forth from

36

beneath the fire pit! Dr. Eggman rose from the ground in a gargantuan monster called the Egg Dragoon. Since the heroes last saw this vile machine, the doctor had fitted it with several drills and worm-like arms that made it capable of burrowing deep within the ground. As it broke

out into the moonlight,

the Dragoon sent dirt, embers, and the two teams flying through the air in all directions.

"What brilliant luck!" laughed Eggman. "I had hoped to strip this forest of its trees in secret so I could build a new robot factory. But I never dreamed I'd be able to bury you in the process!"

Sonic stood up and faced his enemy, fists clenched. "I'd like to see you try, baldy!"

"Hahahahaha!" cackled the scientist. "Talk is cheap, hedgehog! Even you can't defeat an entire forest!"

As the black dirt shook off the back of the Egg Dragoon, the machine lifted an entire rack of fallen trees on its back, which Eggman could now use as weapons.

Crack! The machine launched one trunk at a shaky Vector and Espio, rolling them on their backs. *Swack!* Another giant log swung through the air at Charmy and Tails, swatting them down like flies. *Thunk!* A third tree careened toward Sonic. The hyper-fast hedgehog dodged the attack just in time, but with this kind of firepower, even Sonic started to worry that Eggman had finally won the day.

>>>>>>>>

Meanwhile, deep within the earth, Knuckles fought to dig
his way out. Digging was one of Knuckles' specialties, but for
some reason he couldn't seem to find his bearings.

"Which way is up already?" he yelled as he sank deeper and deeper into the darkness.

With his hands furiously clawing at the earth in front of him, Knuckles suddenly broke through into an empty space. He tumbled forward in an empty, windless hole and landed in the middle of a pitch-black tunnel.

As he stood up, Knuckles saw that the tunnel was round. Roots hung from the ceiling like stalactites in a cave.

Unfortunately, he was not alone.

"Cutter!" came a whisper from deep in the darkness. "Slasher! Ripper!" The words were spit like an accusation.

"Whoever you are, come out!" Knuckles called. "I've had a bad night, and I'm in the mood to punch something!"

Like the flicker of a candle, a soft white light appeared down the tunnel and floated closer and closer. All the while, its tiny voice shrieked, "Cutter! Slasher! Ripper!"

Knuckles squinted in the darkness, and he finally saw it—a small floating body with wavering arms and a large, lumpy head. The creature's face was twisted like the knots on a tree trunk, with big black eyes and a mouth twisted into a horrible gaping hole. It looked like a ghost.

"Slasher! Biter! Breaker!" it called to him and began to swoop and swing around his head.

"Stop it!" cried Knuckles. "Stop saying that stuff!" He swung his arms wildly about, but they never seemed to connect.

Finally the glowing creature floated firmly in front of Knuckles, and he punched at it as hard as he could. But his fist went straight through. All he could feel was bitterly cold air as he sunk his hand into the ground. And with that, the spook flew away.

"Come back here!" Knuckles cried and ran after it. All along the way he punched and kicked at the dirt, but it did no good. Eventually, Knuckles came to a dead end, and the spook hung there, staring right through him.

"The Cutter must be judged!" it hissed. "Take it to the queen!"

From out of the walls, tiny worm-like lights emerged and sunk themselves into Knuckles' skin. They flowed in and out of his face, and he could feel them sliding through his cheeks like icy needles. "Stop! Stop it!" he cried, but the worms seemed to weaken him, and a pair of roots reached down from above and pulled Knuckles into the dirt.

He went limp, and the earth carried him along for what

felt like ages. Knuckles' heart pumped with pure fear until the ground seemed to belch him up into another dirt cavern. This one was lit all around by glowing spooks who hung in a massive network from roots along the dome ceiling. As Knuckles stood up and shivered, he saw the center of the root system made a kind of throne upon which sat a spook that was as big as he was.

She had a long, slender face, but her eyes were deeper and blacker than anything he had ever seen. While she sat lightly in the throne, strands of ethereal light hung off her like cobwebs and connected back up into the earth.

"This is not the one we fight," said the queen spook.

"You got that right! It's Eggman you want!"

"But," said the queen. "This one does not respect our kind."

"What do you mean?" Knuckles said.

She floated down to his level, the strands of her body stretching all the way back to the throne. Then the queen reached out and plunged her ghostly fist straight into Knuckles' heart.

In an instant, he felt it all. These were the spirits of the forest, long forgotten by man. And the one he met in the tunnel was a young spirit—barely five decades old—who took root in the tree he had punched during his fit of anger.

"You, you all feel it," Knuckles said. "And you're all dying. While Eggman tears up the forest, the giant tree at its heart gets weaker and weaker."

"Not just him," said the queen. "You have been cutting and chopping this ancient forest for years. Eggman has just accelerated a long, slow, inevitable end."

Knuckles' eyes opened wide with anger. "I'm sorry," he said. "I'll stop him. With your help, I'll stop it all!"

Across the forest, Eggman had Sonic and his friends on their last legs. His Egg Dragoon stomped and slashed its way through the forest after them.

"Hit him head-on!" called Sonic.

Vector chomped hard at the Dragoon's feet to no effect. Espio began throwing kunai—but they were thwarted by a swinging trunk. Tails and Charmy flew around and around Eggman's cockpit but couldn't get close enough to land a blow.

"The forest can't take much more of this!" called Vector. "And neither can we!"

"Give up, you weak little beasties!" cried Eggman with a maniacal grin. "Nothing can get in my way now."

In the distance, Sonic could see a giant, ancient tree rise above their heads. Its branches swayed in the starlight as if the tree knew what was coming for it.

With a mighty crash, the Dragoon tossed another massive tree to the ground, toppling the team with the force of its landing. Eggman powered on toward the old tree.

But just then, the ground began to shake. Sonic and the team craned their necks to see what was happening, just as the earth opened up to let Knuckles rise from within.

"This stops now!" cried the echidna with fury.

"Ha!" laughed Dr. Eggman. "Does a spiny little bully think he really has the power to stop me?!?"

"Not only can I stop you," Knuckles said, "but I don't even need to touch you to do it!"

Knuckles raised his hands, and from underneath him, an army of ghost lights rose up from the ground and swirled all around him. They flew at Eggman as a thousand tiny voices screamed, "Cutter! Slasher! Ripper!"

The evil doctor's eyes went wild as strands of spectral energy wormed their way through his cockpit and began to crawl in and out of his face. The spirits howled and twisted their features in terrifying shapes. They surrounded him completely, and all Eggman could do was swat at nothing.

"Get away! Get away! What madness is this?" he cried and blasted open the hatch. Eggman tried to crawl to safety, but the spirits were unrelenting. He slipped and fell off the top of the Dragoon, and in midair, the long finger-like branches of the old tree reached out and plucked him. Like a disembodied hand, the tree grasped the villain firmly, then flung him across the forest and into oblivion.

45

With that, the spirits calmed. They floated gently down toward Knuckles, where one small spirit in particular floated just above his eyes.

"Thank you," he said. "I'll keep fighting."

And then they rose up into the branches of the ancient tree and winked away like dying campfire embers.

"That," said Tails, "is going to make for one awesome ghost story."

As dawn broke over the forest, Sonic and Knuckles stood near the edge of the giant tree's root system.

"The old girl looks pretty good," said Sonic. "Eggman did damage, but at least he didn't destroy her."

"Not yet," said Knuckles. "But every day we let this world abuse a forest like this, we bring it closer to extinction. I wish you could have felt what I did when I met the queen of the spirits, Sonic."

"If I didn't know you better, Knuckles, I'd say you sound scared right now."

"I'm not scared, Sonic," he said. "I'm haunted."

HUNT OF THE WEREHOG

The shadowy monster crept into view and slashed its arms out toward Sonic the Hedgehog's face. In the dark and dirty corners of a city alley, it was hard to tell where the black of night ended and the creature began. But one thing was clear: The monster had terrible fangs and was biting forward with all its might. "SKREEEEEE!" the creature shrieked its ear-splitting cry as it lunged right up in Sonic's face . . .

And then the screen cut to black.

Sonic, Tails, and Amy stood in silent shock at the video they'd just watched.

"This was taken last night not three blocks from my laboratory," said Professor Pickle. "And while it is the first definitive proof that these Dark Gaia Minions have reappeared, we've been receiving reports of attacks for almost two weeks!"

"Dark Gaia?" said Sonic. "That ancient monster was as annoying as he was butt-ugly!"

"It's no laughing matter," said Amy. "Last time that creeper broke free, he nearly destroyed the whole planet!"

"Quite," said the professor. "As a hyper-energy organism birthed at the dawn of time, Dark Gaia is an immeasurable, unfathomable power that can pose a great threat to the planet. His minions' reappearance raises the question: Has the monster somehow reemerged from his ancient slumber?"

Sonic zipped around the lab at hyper speed. "If that lord of destruction is back, I'll swat him down like the first time we clashed," said the hedgehog as he skidded to a stop.

"Sonic, you've got to do more than show off," said Amy. "I only saw the Dark Minions from a distance, and I know that they can have a serious effect on people!"

"Ah, you're worrying over nothing, Amy," said Sonic. "The

48

only effects of Dark Gaia's energy were that I got a bit furrier. And these little monsters are probably just stragglers, and we took them out before with little more than a flashbulb camera. Right, Tails?"

The fox had been studying the video footage closely. "Well, I have been tinkering with a better light-based gadget to help destroy Dark Gaia's minions since our first

encounter . . . a kind of super camera," he said.

"Way past cool!" said Sonic. "So let's you and me hit the street and blast these beasties off the map!"

"You better get started, quickly," said Amy, looking out the window. "The sun is going down as we speak and when that happens, the Dark Minions will come out."

"Night or day, there's no way I can't . . . I can't . . . AYYYYYOOOOW!" cried Sonic as his body began to shake. As the sun fell below the horizon, a strange purple smoke rose up from the floor and enveloped the hedgehog. His eyes bulged in pain. His teeth and quills throbbed, then grew in size.

The tips of his fingers sprouted thick black claws through his gloves. And in a moment, the hero had somehow morphed into a monster himself.

"Sonic the Werehog!" cried Amy with fear. "You're . . . you're not supposed to be like this!"

"What's happening to me, professor?" Sonic growled as he flexed his shaggy arms.

"Astonishing!" cried Professor Pickle. "It seems returning to my city and coming closer to this new wellspring of Dark

Gaia energy has reignited your Werehog form. You were always able to resist being fully taken by the darkness, but it appears that your long transformation left you susceptible to the monster's energy."

"Maybe Dark Gaia has returned," said Tails.

"If that's true, then things are about to get a lot more exciting," said Sonic. "Let's go!"

"Wait!" said Amy as Sonic rushed for the door. "I'm no expert in Dark Gaia, but I think you'll want my help."

"It's too dangerous," said the hedgehog as he leaped out of the lab and into the night. "Come on, Tails! Let's get that gizmo charged!"

"I can't believe I'm saying this, but slow it down, Sonic," called Tails. "This thing is heavy!" The fox flew up behind his friend equipped with the Dark Minion–blasting invention he called the flash-banger. The device consisted of a golden power cell Tails wore like a backpack, and from there, cords wound down his arms to two massive gauntlets. Each made his hands into bulb-like fists that could blast a beam of concentrated light. On Tails' wrist was a small screen that recorded images of his targets to steal their power.

"What good is that thing going to be if we can't find any of these Dark Minions, Tails?" said Sonic as his eyes scanned the skyline. "If they were really here in force, we should have found something, *anything* in the city by now!"

"It is far too quiet," said Tails. "But if you're still in Werehog mode, there's got to be something out there."

"Where? This transformation makes me feel so itchy. It's like I've got fleas, but there's nothing!"

"It's almost as if the minions have gone into hiding. That's not their style at all."

At that moment, an eerie scream rang out in the distance of the cold night. It sounded like someone was equal parts terrified and in horrible pain.

"That could be . . . something?" said Tails.

Sonic sped down the hill at top speed. His newly gray fur rippled with anticipation as he lumbered forward.

The scream was coming from a small square barely lit by flickering streetlights. As Sonic zeroed in, he saw a young woman bent over and pulling at her own hair.

"It isn't fair! It isn't fair!" cried the woman, her back to the Werehog. "*Aiiiiie!* Can't anyone do something?!?"

"Hey, lady, it's going to be okay," said Sonic as he slowed to a trot and reached a hand out.

She spun around with an angry jerk. "What could *you* possibly know about it?" she yelled. The skin around her eyes was dark with an unnatural shadow, and the woman sank to her knees in despair. "Oh, it's too late!"

All around the edges of the square, purple shadows swirled. Suddenly, Dark Minions began stepping out of the darkness. Their black bodies throbbed with strange neon light. Their empty red eyes twitched. Their bodies formed into the shapes of sharp spikes, slithering tails, and wagging tongues. They were closing in.

"All right, you little slugs," called Sonic. "It's time you let this woman go and crawl back to where you belong!"

The Werehog dove headfirst into the inky black pile of minions and tried to draw them away from the woman. Skittering around the square again and again, Sonic punched the Dark Minions with his newly extended powerful arms.

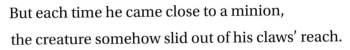

But each time he came close to a minion, the creature somehow slid out of his claws' reach.

"Come out and face me, cowards!" he cried and began swinging. But even with his hyper-extended Werehog arms, the beasts remained frustratingly out of reach. *Fwash! Fwash! Fwash!* Three bursts of light flashed overhead, and the Dark Minions began to reel back and squeal their horrid cries. It was Tails and the flash-banger!

"Don't let them escape, Sonic!" the fox called, snapping the supercharged device.

"Right!" Sonic used his now-extended arms to place all the objects in the square that he

55

could reach at each of the exits to trap the minions.

As the space lit up with Tails' flashes, the minions had nowhere to run . . . except up!

"They're escaping up that building!" cried Tails.

The Werehog used his arms by lengthening them and climbing up the walls quickly, but just as he was about to grab the army of fleeing minions near the building's roof, a bubble of dark energy burst before him like a shadowy grenade. *Shwooom!* The force of the blast hit Sonic hard and tossed the Werehog off the building's side like a rag doll.

Sonic landed on the street below with a crash, and though his Werehog form was strong enough to absorb the impact, his pride took a beating that would sting for days.

"Are you okay?" asked Tails.

"Grrrr . . . I'm fine!" Sonic said, looking up at an empty sky. "Which way did they go?"

"I lost them trying to flash-bang . . . whatever that energy blast was," said Tails. "And I think the sun is about to come up."

"What happened?" asked the woman. She struggled to stand, but her eyes looked clear of Dark Gaia's influence.

"You took a hit from something otherworldly," Sonic said.

"It was so strange," said the woman. "I was out for a pre-dawn run, and I felt this force telling me I was destined to be alone forever . . . like I was the last person left on this planet."

Sonic and Tails made it back to Professor Pickle's lab just as the sun was rising. The effects of the Werehog transformation had worn off, but it had left Sonic wiped of all energy.

"I just need to recharge my batteries, and then we'll track down those minions and figure out what they're up to," he said.

"It's the second part I'm worried about." Tails yawned as he flipped through the images on the flash-banger's screen. "They've never been quite this tricky. It makes me think Dark Gaia has returned."

"Perhaps not," said Amy from behind the Gaia manuscript. "But he may be close to resurfacing." The usually bouncy pink hedgehog dragged herself over to the other two, and the pair could see deep rings underneath her eyes.

"I've been up all night reading the professor's ancient Gaia manuscript," she said. "I wanted to find the secret to what's happening, and I think I have something."

"Come on, Amy," said Sonic, patting his pal on the shoulder. "That moldy old manuscript is full of double-speak and weird riddles. Don't drive yourself crazy trying to figure them out."

"But I really think I have something!" she said. "What I think the manuscript says is that while Dark Gaia slumbers, his extant energy can sometimes scour the planet in search of its master. If the Dark Minions are attacking people, it may be because they're looking for someone to take the place of their lord!"

"Then who is this?" said Tails, dropping the flash-banger's view screen on the table. The picture was of the rooftop where Sonic had been blown back. Thanks to Tails' burst of light, the team could see the Dark Minions retreating over the ledge, but there was something else. A shadowy figure seemed to stand on the roof, calling the minions back with a blurry wave of its arm.

"Whoa!" said Sonic. "Good catch, pal. There's some

mastermind behind this whole scheme after all. But do you think Dark Gaia could have returned at this small a size?"

"It could be him," said Tails. "He may have taken a different form until he can consolidate his energies again."

"But," said Amy with a yearning voice, "my research says that's not possible!"

"Don't sweat it, Amy," said Sonic as he headed off to bed. "Your hammer comes in handy for bashing the occasional robot, but leave this spooky stuff to the professionals."

After a day of fitful sleep for Sonic and Tails, night descended on the city once again. But there was a strange energy in the air as the moon rose, and Sonic felt it as he transformed back into the Werehog.

"There's no second chances tonight," he told Tails as they hit the streets. "I can feel it in my bones. I wonder if we can really seal Dark Gaia again."

And the Dark Minions were out in force. As Sonic sped through the city streets, the inky beasts seemed to taunt him along with the everyday citizens whom they possessed at every turn. Everywhere, people were crying out, "What's the point? We're all so alone!"

At each turn, Sonic would swoop in to save citizens while Tails delivered a one-two blast from the flash-banger to shake off the Dark Minions. But the creatures never stayed long after a fight.

"This is infuriating!" Sonic growled as another batch of minions escaped down a sewer drain. "What are these things even trying to do?"

Tails flipped through his screen for any kind of clue. "I'm not sure what they're getting by terrorizing these poor people, but I *do* think I know where they're going!" He pulled up a map of the city that blinked with red lights. "Do you see the pattern here? Every time we drive the minions off, they run toward this older section of town."

"Then let's go smash it!" the Werehog said and shot off toward the outskirts.

As he raced along, Sonic was irritated. It wasn't just the effect of the dark magic that made him a beastly Werehog. He hated not being in control—not being fast enough to bash in a bad guy's face.

"Sooooooonic!" called a strange voice. The Werehog slowed down outside an alleyway that ended in a large pit like the mouth of a cave. "Sooooooooonic!"

"If Dark Gaia wants me, he's gonna get more of me than he can handle!" Sonic said and raced down underground.

Suddenly, he was surrounded! Dark Minions crawled out from every corner of the cave and screeched and squealed at Sonic as he ran. But they didn't attack. Instead, the creatures descended on the mouth of the cave and began clawing at the rocks around it. FWOOOOM! In a second, the entire opening was closed off in darkness.

"Tails!" he said, realizing too late. "Now I'm all alone without the flash-banger's help. So be it."

Sonic worked his way deeper into dark with only the light of the Dark Minions' glowing bodies to guide him. They kept their distance from the Werehog, but up ahead he could see the shadow of their leader standing on some strange altar.

"So you finally came to me, eh, Sonic?" said a voice that was both squeaky and thunderous. "Without me, you would have never found this energy source."

"Well, now that I'm here, I'm going to bust your butt up all over again, Dark Gaia!"

"Hahahahaha!" the leader laughed. "You think I am the dark one? His power is still hidden at this planet's core, but this energy source called out for someone to care for it. And I answered the call!" With a swing of a hammer, the leader leaped up and struck the ceiling. A hole broke open and the minions detected Dark Gaia energy leaking from this place, letting in just enough of the moonlight. "And I, being obsessed with Dark Gaia, came here, too . . ."

"Amy?!?"

Sonic couldn't believe his eyes. His friend was swirling with Dark Gaia energy. Her pupils were a solid black with the low glow of red energy. And her quills rippled with the same power that had turned him into a Werehog.

"Surprised?" Amy said with a wild smile. "The energy of Dark Gaia was calling to you, Sonic. But you ignored it . . . just like you ignored me!"

"Amy, I didn't mean to . . . I . . ." But Sonic didn't know what to say.

"I was obsessed by the Dark Gaia energy as I studied the

62

minions' actions. I had no idea how powerful it truly was. And it brought me here . . ."

"I'm sorry!" said the Werehog. "But whatever this is, it isn't the answer!"

"Oh, it's not?" said Amy, lifting her hands. "Was I not able to study the Gaia manuscript? Was I not able to gather every single remaining minion in one location? Admit it, Sonic! I have more skills than you thought!"

"Okay, okay . . . I should have asked for your help. I shouldn't have done this alone. But what do you want me to do now, Amy?"

"I want you to watch as I do . . . this!" she said and swung her hammer with ridiculous speed at the ceiling. Pieces of the ceiling rained down around her before Amy cried out, "Now, Tails!"

Fwash! Fwash! Fwash! Fwash!

From up above, Tails rained down blasts from the flash-banger, and the Dark Minions had nowhere to go. Their screams were brief but sharp as, one by one, the army of monsters saw their power stolen by Tails' machine, and they evaporated into smoke.

Amy floated for a moment in the hole she had created, but as the Dark Gaia energy left her, she fell like a stone into the cavern. Sonic rushed forward to catch her, and as she collapsed in his arms, he realized that he himself was a hedgehog once again.

"Sorry to scare you, Sonic," Amy said. "It was hard to fight off Dark Gaia's influence, but I knew I could beat him if I tried."

"It was crazy for me to doubt you, Amy," said Sonic. "And it would have been easier for you if I asked for your help from the start."

"So . . . you don't think I'm a monster?" Amy asked.

"We can all turn into monsters sometimes," said Sonic with a laugh. "But with friends like you, it's easy to turn back."